Cats Behaving Badly

Written and illustrated by
Deb Harris

Thank you to Jacqui, Seb and Ian for making the stories.

Contents

Chapter 1. Mowgli and Mischa meet

First, you need to meet the badly behaved pair.

Mischa is a cute cream-coloured kitten. She has bright green eyes, big ears and a skinny tail.

Mowgli is twice Mischa's size. He's a stocky brown tom cat and looks just like a teddy bear – everyone wants to cuddle him. Sometimes he purrs approvingly; at other times he simply stares at you, silently. Both cats are Burmese, which means trouble because they behave more like monkeys than cats.

The fun began when the Harris family took Mischa home with them in their car. Strangely, Mischa would lean into every turn, just like a motorbike rider. She was quite unlike any other cat they had ever seen.

If you have ever been in a car with a cat, you'll know most of them hate it. They sit, hunched and sweating, in their cat box, scared of the movement and the unfamiliar noises.

Mischa was different. She seemed to like the moving and rolling, and stared at everyone as if to say, 'Is this what you humans call a roller-coaster?'

But the two cats did not exactly like each other when they first met. This is the story...

Mowgli was sitting in his usual spot at the bottom of the stairs, staring longingly out at all the pheasants and blackbirds. He wanted to play with them, to chase them...

Every day he would look out at his dinner running around on the grass, without ever having to do a thing. Just as he was imagining another swift catch, the family's car rolled into the drive.

The family got out. Seb was carrying a large blue plastic box that had holes in it and a wire door in one side. When he carried the box into the house, he placed it on the hall floor and opened the door. Something round-eyed and furry bolted out!

Mowgli sat upright, his eyes as wide as saucers. He couldn't make out what this creature was and what it was going to do. Then a streak of cream fluff shot across the floor towards him, knocking him over. Mowgli lay on his back, kicking with his rear legs as hard as he could, but the cream ball clung to him.

This strange circling fur ball groaned and made other odd noises, then rolled towards the stairs. The family stood by, laughing so hard that they had tears in their eyes. Mowgli – the big, proud boss cat – was being beaten up by a kitten!

At last, Mowgli managed to get away. He ran through the house to hide inside the sofa. But Mischa had other ideas: she sped after him and launched herself at him once again, taking out his back legs with a feline rugby tackle.

Mowgli doesn't meow like most cats do. Instead he produces long, low moans that sound more like a camel with belly ache.

He let out another yowl as he slid helplessly along the floor in a furry white head-lock. He scrabbled for the side of the sofa with his claws, tore loose of Mischa, and ran away. Again.

After hiding for a few hours under the bed, Mowgli crept out, in great need of a snack. Slowly he made his way through the house to his silver dish. This was probably the thing Mowgli loved most in the world – especially when it was full.

His tummy rumbled as he trotted along, looking for the kitten around every corner. 'I really need a bite to eat after such a traumatic day,' he thought.

He needn't have worried about where Mischa was. As he entered the kitchen, there she was, standing over his dish, licking out the very last lumps of gravy and jelly.

Mowgli couldn't believe his eyes. All he could hear was her little tongue rasping against the metal. She didn't even bother to look around at him! What should he do? Should he run away, or stay and get very angry? He would show her who was boss.

Er, no, perhaps he wouldn't, he decided. Instead, he would take a little nap.

Mowgli found a nice napping spot in the airing cupboard. It was always just a little too warm in there, and the dark bothered him a bit when the door was shut, but it would do for today.

After a pleasant nap, he made his way down the stairs to his favourite pheasant-watching spot. 'I'll stop off for a snack on the way,' he thought. 'Sleeping always makes me hungry.'

To his absolute horror, Mischa was there again! She was sitting, bold as could be, on his bottom stair. This was too much. Who on earth did this kitten think she was? Mowgli skulked away, thinking hard. He had to do something! He needed a quiet place to think and hatch a plan.

Sadly, Mowgli wasn't the cleverest of cats. Even though he thought as hard as he could, no brilliant plan came to him.

So he fell asleep.

At least he was in his other favourite place, on the little square of carpet just above the warm water pipes.

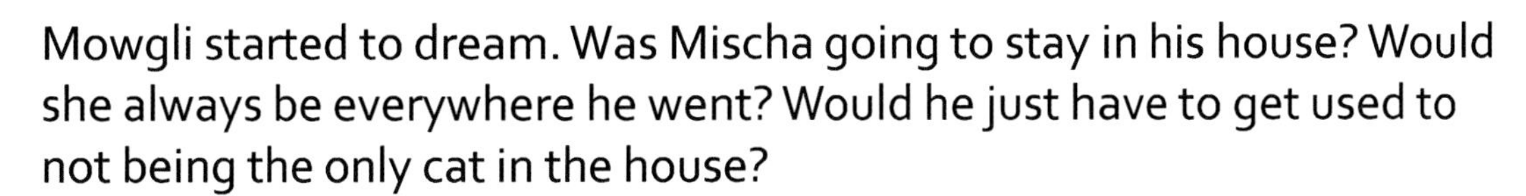

Mowgli started to dream. Was Mischa going to stay in his house? Would she always be everywhere he went? Would he just have to get used to not being the only cat in the house?

After his nap, it was time for Mowgli to have a little fresh air – something he was never that keen on. Maybe his friend Alfie, the black and white cat from next door, would be around for a chat?

But the weather was cold and Alfie was nowhere to be seen. Mowgli wanted to get back indoors. After only a few moments in the garden (and a very quick wee), he jumped in through the cat flap and started up the stairs.

But – oh no! She was there again, sitting on his square of warm carpet. Those water pipes were warming her bottom, not his! It was more than Mowgli could take. He smacked Mischa hard on the nose with his paw. Mischa, who was fast asleep, woke with a jolt and jumped to her feet, her tail standing on end like a toilet brush. She ran away fast.

Mowgli took his rightful place on the comfy carpet, feeling extremely pleased with himself. 'That'll teach the little monkey,' he thought as he dozed off again.

Chapter 2. Mischa and the roses

Mischa was settling in to life in the Harris house quite comfortably. She had three favourite places to sleep. The first was in the warm airing cupboard on top of the towels.

The second was buried deep between the cushions in the window seat downstairs.

And the third was on Jacqui's bed, her body stretched out to catch every bit of sun. Mowgli slept anywhere he could find that was away from Mischa.

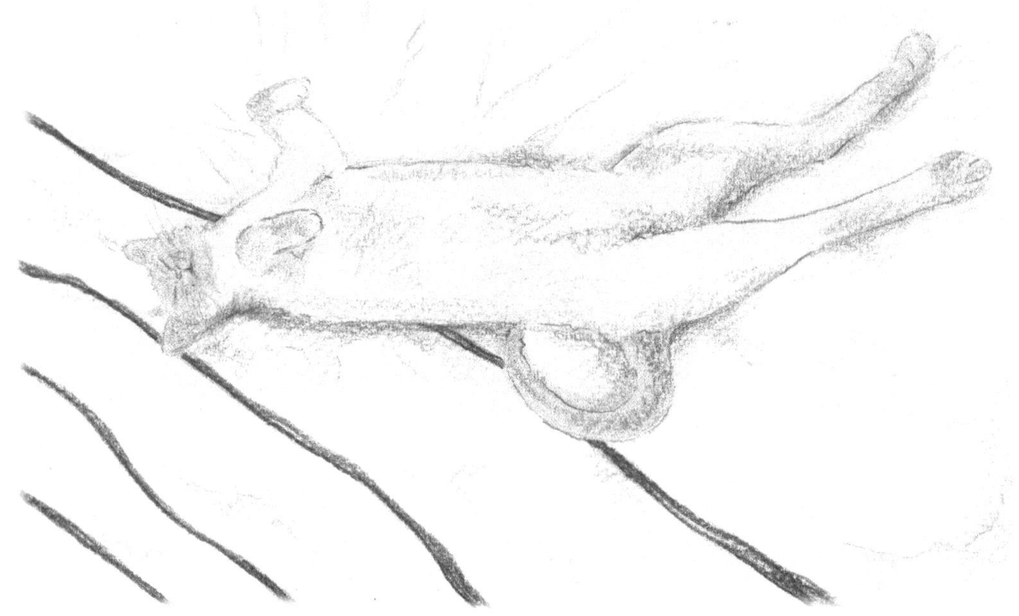

The moment Mischa appeared, Mowgli disappeared! He skulked away with a hiss, then gave a squeaky growl that grew higher and higher. Mischa didn't realise he was scared of her; she simply cocked her head to one side, jumped at him and tried to get him to play. Mowgli would then shoot in the opposite direction before exiting the house at top speed through the cat flap.

Mischa was lonely with no other cats to talk to. She needed something to do – something to keep her busy. Then she spotted some flowers. Mrs Harris loved flowers of all types – roses, orchids, carnations, delphiniums, stocks; the list was endless.

Carefully she arranged blooms of every colour and smell and placed them in vases all around the house.

One day, not long after Mrs Harris had finished arranging one of her most prized rose collections in a vase in the upstairs window, Mischa appeared from a long afternoon snooze. The perfect dark yellow and orange roses sat neatly in a vase alongside white daisies and wispy ferns.

Mischa sat staring quizzically at the flower stems. 'They look just like my chicken treat sticks. Hmm, there are lots of them. I wonder if they're tasty too?' she thought.

The vase was right under her nose – and the flowers were irresistible. She got to work.

A little while later Mrs Harris came back upstairs to make the final adjustments to her flowers. Humming contentedly, she turned the corner onto the landing, scissors in hand.

Oh, what horror! Instead of the twelve perfect rose buds she had left in the vase, several jagged green stalks greeted her. They poked out sadly from the vase, all in a line, almost as if they had been cut by the scissors she was holding. The rose heads were scattered around. Some lay on the windowsill. Others were strewn over the floor. Oddly, the rest of the arrangement was untouched.

This was not the only mysterious incident involving Mischa and roses. A week or so later, the same thing happened again. Mrs Harris discovered a vase full of stalks one afternoon, with flower heads sitting underneath it. This time it was a bunch of pink roses that had been beheaded.

Needless to say, Mrs Harris was devastated, and darling little Mischa was not the first culprit the family thought of. Of course, Mowgli knew it was Mischa all the time. 'If only I could just tell those silly humans,' he thought with a yawn.

However, one Saturday morning Mischa was caught red-pawed – she was spotted gnawing a stem! The family was shocked. Mischa was told off and put outside.

Mr Harris had the perfect solution. 'We should cover the stems in hot chilli sauce; that'll stop her,' he said with a wicked grin.

So the next time Mrs Harris bought roses, she carefully coated them in sauce, as hot as hot can be.

The trap was set.

Another vase of beautiful flowers sat on the upstairs landing windowsill, complete with added sauce. Blissfully unaware, Mischa sneaked up to the vase and took a bite out of one of the juicy long green stems. 'Eat me!' it was shouting at her. Suddenly, her mouth was on fire!

She hurtled off the windowsill, ran up one curtain, across the curtain pole and down the other side, then repeated the circuit twice more, shaking her head furiously and sticking out her pink tongue.

Oh, how Mowgli laughed when he saw her run!

Mischa soon learned to avoid rose stems – until Mrs Harris stopped painting them with the sauce, then the whole circus started up all over again!

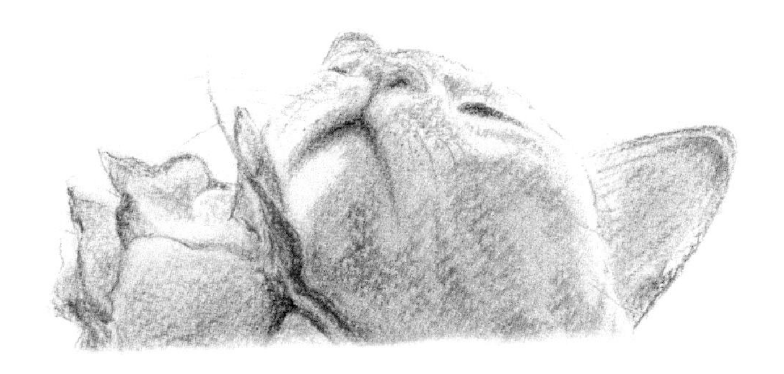

Chapter 3. Mowgli, Mischa and the crisps

Every week, the Harris family went shopping. They arrived home with a car full of big bags. This week, Mrs Harris carried in the bags, ready to be unloaded. They were full of vegetables, meat, bread – and some goodies.

Mowgli and Mischa knew the routine, and often hung around the kitchen to check that their food had arrived safely. Mowgli sometimes wondered if the family had to catch it. He couldn't understand why he never saw any boxes on legs running around outside...

After he had checked the boxes were there, Mowgli went out for a stroll. Sneakily, Mischa helped herself to some dried cat food. The plastic pot of cat biscuits sat on a high shelf. This was no problem for Mischa: she simply butted it with her head until it fell to the floor and spilled the biscuits across the tiles. She promptly jumped down and ate her fill. 'Easy peasy,' she thought.

She often enjoyed a snack this way – it was far more fun than hanging around waiting for a human to decide she was hungry. Besides, she would often meow and wait by the biscuits to try to communicate that she was starving, but the humans took absolutely no notice of her.

This week, Mischa noticed something new. It was a huge red packet on the shelf next to the pot of cat biscuits. It smelled good. It was worth investigation, she decided.

The following morning, the alarm clock buzzed everyone into action.

After breakfast, Mr Harris was making sandwiches for lunch.

'Can someone bring me in some crisps from the top shelf next door?' he called.

Nobody answered, so Mr Harris went through to collect the crisps himself. 'This way,' he thought, 'I can choose my favourite flavour – smoky bacon – to enjoy with my lunch.'

But when he reached the utility room, what a shocking mess he saw! Instead of the crisps sitting on the high shelf, opened packets were scattered across the floor.

The multipack had sixteen bags, all different flavours. Twelve of the bags were still sealed, but all four of the smoky bacon ones had been torn open! Trails of bacon crisp crumbs were strewn over the floor.

'Surely Jacqui and Seb haven't had a midnight feast of smoky bacon crisps?' Mr Harris thought, confused.

At that moment Mischa came trotting through the kitchen. Looking pleased, she pounced on one of the sealed bags of crisps. She bit into the bag and pulled hard until it popped open. Mr Harris looked on, amused.

A quick sniff revealed that the crisps smelled of cheese ... and something else that was unfamiliar. 'Well, that's simply not good enough for a cat to eat,' thought Mischa.

Returning from his stroll, Mowgli stopped dead when he saw what Mischa was doing. He watched in amazement and then sniffed at the opened bag. He turned his nose up too.

Mr Harris couldn't help but chuckle to himself. He decided he would have salt and vinegar crisps for lunch. 'Why do we have to hide everything in this house?' he thought.

Then Mowgli decided he would really like some smoky bacon crisps – and that Mischa shouldn't have scoffed the last pack without offering him any.

A scuffle broke out. Mowgli leapt on Mischa, nipping at her ear. Mischa yelped and sprang high into the air. Startled, Mowgli jumped back and ran away. Mischa sped after him, hot on his tail.

'Watch out, they're at it again!' shouted Mr Harris.

Chapter 4. Mowgli has a plan

Mowgli was sitting in his favourite pheasant-watching spot, daydreaming. As usual, he was thinking about food. The thing that was not usual for Mowgli, though, was that he was thinking very hard. He was particularly hungry today. All of a sudden, he had an idea. It was a fantastic plan, but – and this was a real problem – it involved Mischa.

Dare he go and ask her?

The Harris family were enjoying a lazy Sunday afternoon by the fire. It was cold outside. Seb had come in, fed up with playing football by himself, and Jacqui had her nose buried in a Harry Potter book.

Suddenly, a noise that sounded like elephants thundering across the plain came from upstairs. The family looked around at one another with puzzled expressions, then raced upstairs to see what was happening.

At one end of the hallway sat Mowgli, all fluffy and bright-eyed and looking pleased with himself. They could just see Mischa's paw reaching out from behind a door at the opposite end of the hall. 'Surely they're not playing together?' thought Mrs Harris in disbelief.

Then, in a flurry of red and brown, a large, round pheasant flapped across the hall.

Now, for those of you who don't see pheasants regularly, they're brown, about the size of a large chicken, and have beautiful bright green feathers on their small head.

They have stubby legs and a long striped tail. They are manic birds that are very poor at crossing roads.

They are certainly too large to fit easily through a cat flap! So how on earth had this one got into the house?

The family watched and tried to work out what had happened.

Mowgli tapped at the bird as it came close to him, sending it flying down the hallway to Mischa, who did exactly the same with her outstretched paw. The pheasant squawked, turned back and ran. It was like watching a game of tennis – with a panicking pheasant as the ball.

'How on earth did they get it through two cat flaps?' asked Seb in amazement, a vision of Mowgli pulling at one end and Mischa pushing at the other coming into his head.

Then Seb jumped out and tried to grab the bird. It dodged, and he fell over an excited, leaping Mowgli. The pheasant flapped wildly about, pecking poor Mr Harris on the head. He lunged away and tripped, falling sideways against the wall. Mrs Harris ran wildly around with her precious flowers, desperate to keep them safe. Jacqui watched the chaos and collapsed in a heap, laughing.

For the next half hour the family chased the bird around the house, from one room to another. The pheasant must have remembered the trauma of being pushed and pulled through two cat flaps, because it certainly didn't want to go back out that way!

Finally, Mr Harris caught it under a box and took it outside to release it into a nearby field.

The bird hardly had a feather out of place. Even so, nobody had ever seen such a cross pheasant before.

Inside, Mowgli and Mischa sat side by side in the window, partners in crime. They looked disdainfully at the family, as if to say, 'How dare you spoil all our fun?'

The family had no idea that this was just the start of two cats behaving very badly!

18328944R00023

Printed in Poland
by Amazon Fulfillment
Poland Sp. z o.o., Wrocław